the rooms have you now

a novelette

by

eric danhoff

A quiet voice spoke in between the splitting headache.

"Please allow me to welcome you."

Felix opened his eyes after what felt like an eternity. The office building remained unchanged. It carried the same whitewashed walls. The carpet was still bland and uninspired. The windows where he often looked out retained their same distance from his desk. They were always close enough to inspire thoughts of escape. Despite the sky beyond, the windows were too far to allow him to make the bold exit he had envisioned on a daily basis. It became a routine of sorts to walk by those windows and stare out into the streets. They were never short of people walking back and forth along the concrete. Their bodies moved aimlessly from the beautiful viewpoint the windows had offered. Their little bodies were too small to follow. The distance was too great to see the destination. They would always disappear from his limited sight. His desk looked still frame, untouched since he left it last night. The computer screen was turned off. The black glass reflected the lights of the room, along with a twisted and bent face. Something felt odd about this moment, he thought. He felt separated from his body as he pulled away from the cubical which he had occupied for almost three years. The workplace was forever locked in a constant state of oblivion since his employment began. Today was different. Everything was quiet. No one seemed to be away from their desks. The silence was absolute and it unsettled him.

There was sharp pain when he tried to recall the day's events. He struggled to remember last night. He racked his brain to remember even the day before. Felix attempted to ignore the ache. He gave up and blocked the thoughts from his mind to stop the pain. His clothes were different.

"I've never worn this shirt before", he thought to himself.

"It looks great."

His wardrobe was all black, sharply tailored, as if it was made exactly for him. The business tie was a crimson red. It looked too perfect. None of the clothing he wore brandished the landscapes of white speckles of dirt or fuzz. The clothing was custom made. It was too fine, too perfect. His shoes were a solid black. There were no scuffs or scratches from dragging feet against the concrete of the city outside. He seemed calm for a moment as he admired his new uniform. He made a mental note to complete the day without corrupting these new clothes. A few minutes of solitude passed and Felix began to worry about someone noticing him not working. He poked his head out of the cubicle to see if anyone had moved. It was so quiet he wondered if the day had really begun. His eyes moved across the room. Every head looked to be buried in their computers. There was a sudden rise in the busy clatter of fingers on the keyboard. He furrowed his brow, confused, and sat back down. There was no noise again. He shuffled in his chair. The tweeds of his pants rubbed together and hissed. He began to stare at his desk.

Everything had been moved or cleared away. The computer looked back, reflecting his dark, 120 pound frame and the white shine of his bifocals against fluorescent light. He began to search through his drawers and found that each one was empty. Felix began to notice things missing; the calendar, the clock, pens and pencils. He frantically tore open the other drawers and found nothing. He stood up and looked around, trying to find the clock in the office. There was no clock in sight. He left his cubicle and began to look behind the corners of the office. He had to know what day it was, what time it was. It seemed so odd that his desk was empty, that there was no way to tell the time or the day. Was I being fired? he thought. Maybe the office is being closed down? He walked down the corridors of the room, trying to find some kind of clock or calendar. There was nothing. The silence of the room began to fill Felix with fear. He reached his windows at the end of the hall and looked down at the workers once again. He turned to face the office. He looked around at what cubicles were open from his sight. He finally saw people. They were sitting, typing and looking buried in work. Felix began to walk down his aisle to return to his desk but something stopped him. Returning to the same spot, he looked again at the other workers. He looked at their clothes and realized they were dressed in black as well. He studied his own uniform and glanced again at the nearest person. Their clothes were exactly the same.

They had the same black shirt and pants, the same crimson tie, the complete lack of wear or wrinkles. He approached the man closest to him. He was like the others, his face and hands transfixed on the computer screen. He didn't notice Felix walking towards him. No papers or notes, no clock, no pictures. He tapped the man on his shoulders, expecting him to turn his head, or speak.

"Hello?"

No answer. He called again, still no response, his eyes stayed on the computer, Felix looked at his hands as they typed with frantic energy. He could hear quiet sobs. Felix felt his heart stop. He called his name again, still no answer. Felix began to look at his computer screen, a word document open, the words *"Don't Remember,"* repeated over and over. There were no spaces between the words. He grabbed the man's shoulders.

"Are you alright?"

He turned him around. He wanted to see his face. The man was crying. His eyes were completely white. Tears ran down his face to his black clothes. Felix looked to see the tears left no spots of moisture, no mark at all.

"What the hell?" Felix asked, frozen.

He backed away suddenly. The man looked at him sobbing uncontrollably. He repeated the words on his computer screen. Felix slowly backed away from the desk. The man continued crying and repeated the words again and again as he slowly turned back to the computer. His fingers reached for the keyboard and began typing. Felix stepped forward and stuck his face into the cubicle. There was no eye contact, no pulling the man away from the screen. Felix saw his face had changed. It was now stoic and dry of tears as if nothing had happened.

Felix was stunned. The sudden change in the man's expression frightened him. No one had noticed what just took place. He looked around to see if anyone had heard the commotion or the loud crying. Everyone remained silent at their desks.

"Hello? Did anyone hear that? This man needs help."

No one made a sound.

"Hello?! HELLO?! HEY!!!"

Nothing again. Anger began to overtake the fear. None of these people paid any attention to him. Someone had to have heard that, he thought. Felix looked to the cubicle to the right of the man; there was a woman, a black button shirt tucked neatly into a blood red skirt. He walked up to the woman and pulled her away from the desk.

"Are you listening?" he asked.

Felix let go of the woman's shoulders. The woman 's facial expression was a twisted mess; black scars and cuts scattered across deep bruises a sickly purple, caked with blood. Her right ear was missing. Around her eyes, there was skin missing. Pieces of bones stuck out from both eyebrows. Her flowing red hair was divided to reveal torn skin, open wounds and skull. The woman's eyes were white. Blood ran down from several places on her head, Felix followed it with his eyes. The rivulets traveled down her neck to her shirt, and from there dissipated. Her clothes, as perfect as the crying man, as perfect as Felix's own. The woman shivered and swayed back and forth, fatigued and sleepless.

He turned to investigate the woman's desk; walls barren, drawers completely empty, nothing except for the computer, the words were typed over and over without spaces; "*Don't catch me*", he pressed the -page up- key, the pages went on and on. "*Don't catch me*". She had to have been typing for hours, maybe days even. "*Don't catch me*". He began to scroll faster, the pages continued on without end, 100, 200, 3 to 400 pages. "*Don't catch me*". He stopped himself and returned to the woman, who remained standing the entire time, almost as if she had no control over her own body.

"Don't worry, I'll find help for you. Just stay here," he said.

Felix carefully placed the woman back into her chair and pushed her to the desk. The woman slumped over in her chair with no energy, no life. Felix stepped away from the desk. He began to walk away and stopped again when he heard the clicking of the keyboard. He turned back towards the woman. The right ear which looked like it had been ripped away, was now there in perfect condition. She was typing again, sitting upright. Felix moved over to see into the cubicle and saw that one side of her face was completely healed. There were no traces of blood, no bruises or bone. His jaw dropped. Felix quickly ran back to the woman and pulled her away from the screen to see her entire face had healed. As he pulled her away from the screen, the new skin melted away revealing her true face, destroyed again. Felix let go of the woman, she crawled back toward her screen as brand new skin grew over her wounded flesh.

"WHAT IS HAPPENING?! DOESN'T ANYONE HEAR ME?!"

Felix screamed. The office gave him nothing.

"HELP US!"

No one moved.

WHAT IS WRONG WITH YOU PEOPLE?!"

There was still nothing.

"DAMN IT!!"

Felix looked around at every worker in the office. He ran down the middle row, past the broken woman and the weeping man and pulled the chairs out from the adjacent desks, trying to grab the attention of these people. Felix pulled a group of five away from their screens. He yelled and screamed to wake them up, only to watch each of their faces turn shades of white and green. They began to decompose as they crawled back to their computer. Felix continued running through the office. He grabbed every person and watched them deteriorate away from the desk. Frustration ran through his body. Thoughts flooded his mind.

"What the hell is happening? Were they dead? They can't be alive. What is this?"

Felix tried to remember the day before, what got him here. He didn't remember coming to work, driving through bad traffic like every morning. He couldn't remember the news, the tacky songs of morning rock radio, the sunlight pouring through his windows. He couldn't recall that same burning red sunlight. He didn't remember the dream of the night before. He couldn't remember waking up at all.

"This is a dream", he laughed.

"This has to be a dream."

Felix felt a sharp stab of pain in his right temple. He tried to remember but the pain grew worse, he couldn't think of anything. He couldn't remember his life, his last name, where he lived, his phone number. The migraine grew in size, until Felix fell to his knees from the pain, still he tried to recall whatever memories he could.

"What city do I live in? Where was I born? Where are my parents?"

One last stab of pain and Felix fell to the floor. He could remember nothing. The mind was overcome with pain. His eyes began to blur. Felix looked up to see figures approaching and he cowered away. He crawled to the window and found that one spot that he looked to for escape. At least what he thought he looked for. He wanted to escape that feeling. It weighed on him like a prone body. The figures came closer. Felix's eyes settled on what was a single man, dressed in white. His hands reached down towards him, Felix screamed in fear, until the hands had comforted him and helped him to his feet; The man was smiling.

"What is this? Where am I?" whimpered Felix.

One of the men spoke softly, almost angelic.

"Please allow me to welcome you. As you can see we are very busy here, hence no proper introductions. Forgive us, but we welcome you nonetheless."

Felix quivered underneath the man, hands shaking and fearful. His breath shortened and returned to normal as he rose slowly to his feet, the man in white helped him.

"What do you mean busy? These people are hurt, something has happened to them, we have to do something."

"There is nothing that needs to be done, friend. Please allow the others to continue their work. You have work to do as well. Please find your way back to your desk and begin."

"What are you talking about? These people are hurt, we have to help or they'll die!"

A second man spoke.

"Please understand. The rooms have you now," they said.

Felix' eyes widened, he was unable to say anything. He was shown back to his desk, one of the men turned his computer on and walked away. Felix could feel his heart beating outside of his body, fast and restless. Something about that man's words, the finality of it, was too chilling. The computer's white screen was bright and clean. He was unsure what to do. Moments later, the typing reticle appeared on screen. Felix grabbed the keyboard and pulled it towards him. He hit one of the keys, a small black q dropped onto the white backdrop. A few moments passed, Felix looked away from the computer at the opening of his cubicle to the hallway. A small, electronic noise sounded and Felix turned his head quickly back to his computer. A question had appeared; the small black text appeared on its own. More fear raced through his veins.

"What is your name?" the question beckoned.

"Felix," he replied.

Seconds passed, another question appeared.

"What has happened to you?"

This question caught him off guard, he could not remember what happened to lead him here, he tried to answer as truthfully as possible.

"I woke up at work, I don't remember much else. Who are you?"

Felix felt his heart beat heavier as each second passed without a reply, he wanted answers, but was too shaken to press forward. The computer finally replied after what felt like hours.

"That's quite alright. That's why I'm here, to help you remember."

Felix replied quickly.

"You didn't answer my question. Why am I at work? What happened to these people? Who are those men in white? What the hell is happening right now?"

The reply came as Felix continued to type, it cut him off mid sentence.

"Hell is exactly right."

"What do you mean?" he asked.

"Meaning, Hell is what's happening right now."

"What?" He smashed the letters into the keyboard.

"This is not your workplace. This is our workplace. These people are like you, dead and in denial."

"Why do they say we are dead? I'm not dead. I'm alive right now, talking to you. I'm not dead."

There was an even stronger silence within the room. The computer took even longer to reply, the waiting hurt Felix badly.

"Yes, you are," was the reply.

Felix shot up from his chair and it flew out into the aisle,

"NO!!!" He screamed at the text on the screen.

"I'M NOT DEAD!!!!! I'M ALIVE!!! DAMN YOU!!!! ALIVE!!!"

Just then, for the first time the people around Felix began to react to him, the noise of frantic typing stopped. Felix' ears picked up on the sound and his heart froze, he looked slowly to his sides to see the heads of his co-workers staring at him. Their skin and eyes melted away as they averted gaze from the white screens.

The skulls stared intently at Felix. The fear was too much and he screamed and put his foot through his computer. Glass and pieces of silicon shattered upon impact. He looked to the others and watched as their heads slowly returned to their work. The skin and blood returned to their bodies, held together by the white light of the computer, and the typing of the keyboard. Felix was then surrounded by the men in white, their sympathetic looks were now more unsettling than ever.

"Sir, please have a seat and collect yourself, everything will be alright, please try to begin your work," he said.

Felix screamed back.

"What work? My computer is smashed."

One of the men pointed towards the desk. Felix looked to see that his computer was just fine. A screen of white ready to begin typing once again. His eyes widened, scared and mentally drained, he took a seat at his computer, The computer asked him his name. Felix replied. The computer asked again.

"What has happened to you?"

Felix looked at the screen, unable to think of anything but an answer. He typed slowly.

"I died, and I am in hell."

He looked back to see the men in white look on and nod in approval. Felix swallowed hard, his nerves wracked as we waited for the next question. He began to feel his head shrink and he closed his eyes in pain. When we opened his eyes, there were words on the screen,

"You were always a pushover, you know."

Felix grimaced, unable to understand the statement. It wasn't a question, it was talking to him. The computer began to speak to him.

"Look at you. There is no fight left in you. There never really was any fight in there, was there? So willing to give up and take your seat at this desk? Not even try to understand why you're here? Why the black clothes? The faces melting? Everyone dead around you? Those angels, so nice and understanding. They are so forgiving. You never deserved forgiveness. You still don't."

He could not wrap his head around the words. He began to feel sharp pains in his neck and head, as if the words were coming from his own mind.

"Look at you; an eternal loser. Continue sitting there, struggling to find reasons to like yourself. So difficult it must be to accept the fact that you're a failure."

The migraines grew in intensity, Felix felt these words before, there was an old stench of familiarity, yet he could not decipher their origin.

"You think you're the only one who can feel pain? You never stopped to realize what you took from me."

Felix strained his eyes as images tore their way into his mind, for the first time. He felt hopeless as the words continued to appear on the screen. Felix lowered his head onto the keyboard as he felt himself falling into the finality of the moment. That's it, he thought, I'm here forever. Facing these words. He closed his eyes and tried to remember. The images continued breaking into his mind. He flinched with every flash. He felt it now. He was dead.

He suddenly felt something grip his skin. He could not move his head like before. The grip hardened. His head was attached to the keyboard, he struggled and with a cry he ripped his head back, he saw the skin, still fastened to the keyboard. He felt his face, there was bone, there was no blood, no skin. He screamed and fell back to the wall of his cubicle, he rolled to the side to escape. He got up and ran away from the screen. Felix looked around the men in white. I suppose they were angels, he thought to himself, that's what it told me. He felt strange referring to the computer as a living thing. Was it a man or a woman? Something else? He felt for his face as his skin was returning to him. He knew the men in white would be returning to politely return him to his chair, he knew that he had to stay. He wanted to run, to escape somehow. He took several steps toward the cubical, then ducked behind the wall to avoid the passing man in white. Felix thought of the window, he wanted to jump out, to fall to the concrete, would it kill him? Again? Just then, he looked up to see a woman in red and black, dressed as he was.

She was staring at him with strange eyes. Felix looked to the floor, then turned to scramble on all fours towards the window. He rose to the window, looking around quickly to see if anyone was approaching. He saw the woman again. She was still staring at him. Her skin was not missing. He quickly turned back to the window. The sun was bright and it blinded him as he pulled at the side of the window. It would not move.

He pulled harder and still nothing. He decided to grab a chair and toss it at the glass. It bounced back and crashed into the cubicle behind him. The man in white stopped and turned. He walked quickly towards Felix. He moved towards the man in white and then turned towards the window and ran towards it. Felix threw himself at the window trying to smash it.His body bounced off the glass, flying further back than the chair and crashed to the floor.

The man in white looked down at him with an innocent smile, and briskly picked him up and carried him back to his desk.

"Here you go, sir. Please try to resume your work."

His attitude angered Felix, who kicked and shoved at the large man holding him over the computer. He looked down to see his piece of skin still there, twitching as though alive. The man's expression never changed despite the violent reactions. He placed Felix down gingerly and walked away. He was trapped, he thought, there was no way out the window, no way to leave the room. Felix looked down at the piece of skin. He closed his eyes, which dripped with tears. He was to accept his situation, see it to the end. He placed his head back upon the keyboard, he felt the grip returning. A wet smooth sensation slipped over the edges of his face. The grip tightened and he felt the liquid pouring over his entire face. A light cool air swept over the wetness. Felix opened his eyes to see his skin peeling off of his face. The wet liquid feeling had been his blood, and his warm flesh meeting the cool air of the room.

His skin was being pulled into the screen of the computer by some unknown force, invisible fingers tearing away his human shell, he felt immense pain. He could not speak. He watched his lips rip away from his head, he opened his mouth to let the air out of his body. He felt the fingers reach for his eyes. The pain increased and wrenched away, pulling the pieces of his face away from the computer screen. The pain was blinding now. He laid his pieces quickly on the desk. His blood poured from the wounds made. His fingers had stopped the flow but the wounds burned as he moved away from the screen. The screen had cauterized his wounds. Desperation overwhelmed Felix as he tried to reassemble his face. He moved beyond fear and disbelief as he moved the pieces together as tight as he could. Felix pressed them to the gaping wound. He fell back from the chair and crawled to the corner of his cubicle. He stayed out of sight from whoever may pass by. He closed his eyes and felt the skin gripping to his flesh.

Felix kept his hands over his face until the skin ceased slipping and finally re-attached. He saw a shadow from the outside of his office. The figure quickly threw a piece of folded paper into the room and it landed on Felix's desk. He crawled towards the desk and looked around the opening. There was no sign of the men in white. He grabbed the paper and scrambled back to the corner. It was folded like a note. It reminded him of high school. Although he never received a note from a girl, he had seen others write and pass on such letters with glee. He opened the folds to see inside. It was writing.

"Hello, how are you? This is a silly question to ask but can you look up for a second?"

Felix raised his eyes to the ceiling and was dumbfounded, maybe it's another person in the office. He raised his head slowly to oversee the surrounding desks. The woman who was staring at him was looking in the same nervous way, her eyes barely noticed over the edge of the wall. They both quickly ducked back down. A few seconds passed, they both raised their heads again, their eyes met, she waived and he returned. They both lowered their heads once more. Felix was unsure of what to do, was she alive? Did she just arrive? Like him? How long was she here? She must have been sitting at her desk this whole time, why is she talking to me? Felix thought. A few moments passed, and then another note flew over the wall and landed in front of him. It was folded like the other one. He opened it.

"What's your name?"

He was confused, why would she want to know? At a time like this? In this hell? He decided it better to gain a friend perhaps amongst this insanity. Though there was little use for a friend in this situation.

Moments before letting his body seemingly pass through the white screen, attaching himself permanently to the text and typing. Where could this go before they had to face this fate in front of them? He had no pens or pencils, unsure of what to use to write a response. He noticed some blood remaining underneath his neck, where his face had returned. He shrugged and collected the blood to his finger, with that he wrote "Felix" in bright red letters that ran down the remainder of the page, folded it back into it's complex shape and tossed it over to the wall where he saw the eyes and brown hair of a woman.

He could remember her face when he tried. He wasn't sure whether to keep the blood on his neck in case of another needed response. A note flew over the wall again, followed by a pen. This made Felix smile immediately. He opened the note and read it.

"Wow. You wrote your name in blood, quite a romantic gesture. You have a cool name as well. Are you Spanish or something? My name is Vespertine. It means "flourishing in the evening," in case you wanted to know. Nice to meet you Felix."

He marveled at the name, Vespertine, he repeated in his head over a few times. That's the most beautiful name for a woman I've ever heard, he thought. He wondered what she could look like as he clicked the pen and began writing.

"Definitely cool. Let no one tell you any different."

Felix laughed. He threw the note and waited. He thought about her name, he wanted to see her face. How would they make contact with the men in white stalking the halls? A few minutes passed, and the note returned. Felix unfolded and read.

"Thanks. I'm going to go out on a limb and say that you and I both don't want to be here. I saw you try to throw yourself out the window. That was pretty brave, you know. Admirable. But listen, I'm going to break out of here. Would you like to come with me?"

The question shocked Felix. It was true that he didn't know what this place was, he said it was hell, but there was no fire or burning or torture. Maybe it was a kind of hell, either way he could not remember why or how we got to this point. He had obscure images and the unsettling words from the white screen. There was nothing else, nothing that could help remember. He did want to escape, but he had no idea how. This place was shaped like an office building, he thought, there must be a door or hallway, a staircase to different floors or something. That thought shook Felix, how many floors could there be? Were they all like this? Do they get worse? Maybe this place really was an office building. He needed to know, there can't possibly be a way to just walk out, but the men in white were so nice and docile, maybe they would let us leave if we wanted to. Felix remembered that through all his kicking and screaming, fighting with them, he never once asked to leave, or simply left of his own choice. How would they react if he did this? He had to know the boundaries of the situation if any sort of attempted escape was to be made. He wrote quickly on the paper and tossed it over to Vespertine.

Felix heard the heavy familiar footsteps of the large man, he must be coming back to check on him, he wondered how just how much time has passed since he left. He got up to a crouching position so as not to be seen before necessary. He thought to ask to leave, or walk out, but he felt that now was not the time. He moved over to his desk. Unsure of what to do, he heard the footsteps approaching. Felix sat down and began typing gibberish on the computer. The white screen displayed letters and symbols that spelled out nonsense. He heard the large man enter the cubicle, he felt his presence just behind him, a looming shadow of white stretched over the black desk. In the midst of typing nonsense, he remembered that each man or woman had some repeated phrase that meant something to them. Without thinking he wrote; "it burns" and then reverted back to the gibberish, only to repeat the phrase again and again in between bursts of random letters.

The man with the white shadow spoke.

"Hmm, different from the others."

Felix kept going until the man stumbled away from his cubicle. Felix then regained his composure, he was more fearful of the men in white with every encounter. Would they become violent when he was found attempting to escape? He thought, Does it even matter? If we're already dead, how would they hurt him? This seemed to make sense to him and gave him more confidence to make a break for whatever lay outside the room. He felt the paper hit the floor, he turned around quickly and grabbed the paper, diving for the corner. He opened it frantically and read the words;

"Sounds like a plan to me, I say we start now, are you ready? Before we do anything, I want to see you face to face, can I come over to you?"

Felix felt a short burst of excitement at seeing her face. He was unsure of how to react. He wrote his reply and tossed it over. He waited. Seconds later, a girl came rolling into the cubical and jumping back into the corner he occupied. She was almost on top of him. He was shocked. She pinned him to the wall to avoid any indication of suspicious activity. She kept her eyes on the opposite wall, waiting for the white shadows to investigate. He could not see her face from this angle. Her brown hair curled and bunched together in the back. Her skin was olive. Felix focused his eyes on her neck. Until she turned her head to speak.

"So sorry, I didn't want them to hear anything, so I jumped in, apparently all over you." She laughed quietly.

Her face captivated him. Her eyes were a deep green. The skin shimmered beneath the fluorescent lighting. There were several tiny black moles around her forehead. Beauty marks. Her lips were pink. White teeth gleaming through her mouth. Felix studied the face, as he spoke. She was too beautiful, he thought.

"That's quite alright, we're here now."

"Yeah, I wanted to see you, because I wanted to ask you again face to face. Are you sure you want to try to escape with me?" she asked.

"Of course, why wouldn't I?"

She looked down.

"I don't know, we just met and I didn't want to freak you out or drag you into something you didn't want to do in the first place."

Felix was taken aback by this but she continued.

"I don't like this place. It scares me. I want to leave and don't want to pressure you into helping me, you may accept this place. If that's the case, let me know and I won't bother you again."

He thought about falling into the white screen. He looked into her eyes.

"You have no idea how happy I am that someone else is here, like me, I want to escape and I will do everything I can to make sure we both leave here."

She smiled.

"Thank you," she said.

There was a slight pause between them. They exchanged looks, both smiled and then carried on.

"Well, what do you think we should do?"

Felix answered.

"This place seems like an office building, the windows are blocked somehow, I think we should look for an elevator or staircase."

Vespertine nodded in approval.

"Sounds good. We should look for one from afar before we start moving around the floor."

Felix agreed and volunteered to look first. He raised his head above the cubical to view the floor. It was massive, with winding halls packed with cubicles like his own. He closed his eyes and reopened them to focus. He followed the windows opposite his side of the room. The back corner held an open doorway. It was far, from his eye, there was only a black square in the wall. It had to be a door. There was a man in white walking calmly around the area. The man turned to view the room, and Felix ducked his head and almost caught the eye of the man in white. He told Vespertine of the door. Her face lit up. They took a minute to collect themselves, then crawled out onto the floor and moved swiftly across the hall. They looked up at times to see the others typing in their spaces. Some were crying, their faces buried in their white screens. Indiscernible text streaming across the monitors. Felix heard the cries. He tried to block them out. He thought that perhaps without Vespertine, he would have been one of them. He tried desperately to remember what happened to him. There was a shock of pain that made him fall to the floor.

He cried out in pain. Vespertine was ahead of him, she stopped and looked behind to see Felix writhing on the floor, she looked forward, they were halfway to the wall. Almost to the end of the room. She grabbed Felix and tried to speak to him. The migraines were massive. Tears poured from his eyes. She held his head and wiped the tears.

"Come on, we're almost there! What's wrong with you?"

She heard footsteps. The man in white had to have heard him.

"I'm not leaving you!" she whispered.

She looked around frantically, waiting for the man to discover them. She saw the white shadow approaching on the corner wall. She dragged Felix into the cubicle next to them. There was a man sobbing into his palms, sitting at the desk. She held Felix and herself against the wall as the white shadow stood around the corner from them. She caressed Felix with her hands. Felix gave up trying to remember. The escape was more important now, he thought. The pain receded. The man at the desk stopped crying. He looked up and turned to see Vespertine cradling Felix. She looked up and saw his face melting away from the white screen that maintained his earthly visage. Her jaw dropped as the skull began peering into her eyes.

Felix watched the white shadow move from the wall. He waited a few seconds, then turned his head to see the man turn the corner. He grabbed Vespertine and pulled her away from the skull. It had detached from the man's body and began to follow her. It began to bond with her face, bone on bone.

She was motionless. Felix fearfully was now dragging her away from the skull. She regained her senses and they resumed crawling frantically down the new hallway. As she moved away from the desk, she heard a voice in her head speak to her.

"Don't turn away."

The black square from afar was now closer, it was a doorway but it was too far to see inside. Felix led Vespertine down the hallway. She was visibly shaken though her face was untouched. Felix was relieved that her beauty was not compromised. He wanted her to remain unharmed. The voices began to enter his mind as well. Voices from all the others. They were calling for help. To stop the pain. To kill them. He closed his eyes and thought of her face. She grabbed his hand and they crawled nervously through the hall. They wanted the voices to stop. They pushed harder and harder until Felix felt the floor surface change. He opened his eyes to concrete. He looked back to see the office. They were in another place. He looked up to see an immense ascending staircase. He led Vespertine to the side and he saw a door sealing off the staircase from the office. He shut it quickly and exhaled.

They both sighed relief and rested. They opened their eyes soon after to view the new surroundings. They felt as though they had been staring at white walls their entire lives. The stairwell was a deep, industrial grey, the stairs traveled upwards and downwards. The red rails followed up and down for what looked to be miles. Each floor held a door. Felix wondered what lay beyond each of those doors. As he rose to his feet, Vespertine held onto his arm,. She pulled herself up along with him. Felix looked up to the next level and began to climb the stairs. Vespertine followed as they climbed the hard concrete steps, there were clamping noises with each step that echoed in the hollow space. The next level was similar in appearance to the bottom. The ominous black door looked down at them.

He walked up the last steps and approached the door. He opened it and saw another office. The hallway was paved with white washed walls that went on to some unknown end. He saw the cubicle. He saw the heads of the workers. He heard the voices, the frantic typing, the cries and screams. Felix ducked behind the wall as a man in white passed his line of sight. He waited for the man in white to disappear, hoping he would not notice the open door. Suddenly, the typing, the voices stopped. He turned back around, peering into the room. The workers were all looking toward the door. They were looking toward him. Their faces melted into the soulless skulls of before, they detached from the heads and moved toward Felix. He was frozen in fear, he tried to move, but could not.

He felt something pulling at his shirt. He was unable to look down to see her olive hands ripping at his immobile arm. Felix heard voices, speaking to him, they spoke with familiarity that startled him;

"Go ahead, pull the trigger."

He remembered a gun in his hands years ago.

"You've never done anything right before. What makes this any different?"

Vespertine was yanking and pulling at Felix. She looked up to see the skulls entering the hallway. They were inches from Felix's face when she slammed the door, knocking the skulls back into the office. The spell over Felix was somehow broken and he fell to the floor.

She pulled him up and helped him down the staircase. They hid underneath the ascending stairs as a man in white opened the door, he had heard the noise and watched the exits, waiting for something to try to escape. Vespertine kept Felix still. He felt her hands caress his neck and face again. Her touch slowed his heartbeat to next to nothing. He smiled. She would never be with me outside of this place, he thought. She was too beautiful. She was outside his grasp. The man in white returned to the office, leaving the door open.

Felix looked into her eyes. She spoke calmly.

"Why don't we try downstairs?"

Felix collected himself and looked down. The way down stretched on forever it seemed. They held hands and began the descent down the endless steps. The levels downward all had open doors. They quickly jumped down the steps and then quickly ran past the opening, trying to avoid being seen, by the men in white, the workers, anything at all. More and more floors passed, each one held another office. Hundreds of people transfixed on their monitors. The white screens that beckoned them to let go, to let themselves be sucked in.

As they ran, Felix thought about that feeling, of losing himself to whatever is out there. He thought of Vespertine. He was happy she found him. He was relieved that she chose him. Maybe they were the only ones on that floor? Maybe there are more people like us in these other offices?

Did they have enough time or energy to search each of these floors? Risking capture or whatever could await them if caught? The voices, the cries and screams were heard faintly as they traveled down the stairwell. They moved fast enough to avoid being caught in the trance again. It seemed the workers were trying to pull them both in. To make us join them, he thought. He remembered the way the skulls tried to graft onto the face of Vespertine, the beautiful woman next to him, running frantically down these stairs. She was his companion. They ran what felt like hours, they had run out of energy and slowed to a walking pace until they finally decided to stop and est beneath the previous staircase to stay out of sight from the upper lever. Felix quietly closed the door leading to the lower level and for a while they were safe to rest.

"How much longer?" Vespertine asked.

She was nearly without breath. Felix laid his head against the concrete.

"I don't know but we have to keep going. Are you ready?" He asked.

She nodded and they continued down the steps. They had to rest many more times. The stairs keep going beyond what they thought it would be. Felix began to fear that the stairwell may as well go on forever. How did we know that it wasn't the same staircase? The same offices and rooms, waiting for us to give up? He gripped hard onto her hand. She returned the grip and they kept going. They lost track of time. They only thought of the stairs. The red rail followed like a spine jutting from the eternal rows of stone. Soon they were practically falling down the stairs, barely keeping each other from crashing down to the concrete. They were both mentally and physically exhausted. They fell to the floor gasping for air. Felix got up slowly, felt a black wave of hopelessness take over. He looked up expecting to see another open office, more stairwell, never ending. Felix saw the white door. It shocked him. He looked around to see there was no lower level. They had reached the bottom. Vespertine crawled over to him and he helped pull her up to her own feet. They looked back and forth between the door and each other. He signaled towards the door. She nodded. He walked towards the door and pushed it open. White light flooded the dark room and they slowly walked outside to the city street.

The street was filled with wandering people. Their faces were tinted with white and shades of yellow as the sun cracked through a heavy barrier of clouds above their heads. Their clothes were different, battered and torn with shades of brown and gray. Felix looked up to see the building they had just escaped. It was a massive skyscraper. A tower of black stone and tinted glass that was even taller than he thought it would be. Felix ran around the building to see behind it. The clouds were thick and flowing. They wrapped around the building and traveled down to the street itself. A dome of sun and sky around the building and it's street. Vespertine grabbed Felix's arm and told him to look around.

The crowds of people seemed to wander to the end of the street, reach the wall of clouds, and then turn around and walk to the other end. Many of them were laid down in the middle of the street. They all looked upward, searching. Some were looking at the building across the street. Felix ran across the street and around the other building to see the same wall of clouds behind the first. They were still trapped somehow, he thought, but anything could be better than what was inside the building; all those screams, the white screens, the stalking skulls. They were safe here. Felix walked around to see Vespertine looking through one of the open windows of the building, she was in a line of people staring blankly at the window. Felix went and stood next to her, she did not notice. He looked at her, then turned to the window. It was some kind of restaurant.

The people were sitting at ornate tables. Beautiful architecture surrounded them, with several golden sculptures. The floors were lined with ivory and silver. In the corners were jade pillars that supported the main room. An amazing glass chandelier swayed above the patrons, who were decorated in spotless white clothes. It resembled a piece of living art. The people moved at a measured pace, calm and collected. They ate from fruit and food that looked as if it were made from ivory as well. Felix was hypnotized. He saw a little girl take a bite from an ivory apple. The inside of the fruit was white as well. Golden juices flowed from the apple's flesh down to her clothes. He saw the juices disappear after making contact with the fabric. The little girl smiled and continued eating. They were wearing clothes like ours, he thought. He and Vespertine looked at each other, they wanted to go in. They wanted to eat from the ivory fruit.

They looked at the group of people around them. Some were scratching at the windows, tapping frantically on the glass, yelling obscenities at the people inside, pleading and begging to let them in. They didn't. They never even turned their heads. We did not matter to them, Felix thought. He wanted inside, for himself and for Vespertine. He found a pane of glass away from the bystanders and began ramming himself into it, trying to break through. The glass was harder than the window of the office building. He continued throwing himself at the glass but it did not matter. The glass was stronger than him. He fell to the floor and clutched his shoulders and sides. He looked to the ground as Vespertine walked towards him. She kneeled down next to him with sadness in her eyes.

"We can't get in," she said.

Felix felt a bit of failure inside.

Vespertine helped Felix to his feet and they walked along the street, away from the crowd of people, she remained silent as he spoke aloud.

"So, I guess we're still trapped on this street, between these two places. There has to be something outside of this. Where did all these people come from? Do you think that they left the office building like we did? If they did, how did their clothes change?"

Vespertine interrupted.

"What do you think is behind the clouds?"

Felix looked at her, and then at the wall of clouds that blocked the street and led up and around the skyscraper. He wanted to know as well. They approached the wall.

Felix moved closer to the wall of white. The wall was nothing but deep fog. He could not see beyond the fog as he grew nearer. There were small bursts of electricity within the flowing swirls. He reached his hand inside the wall and a beam of electricity shocked his hand.

He felt pain, he heard voices. Loud, thunderous voices taunted him. The pain returned. The crippling migraine that appeared when he tried to remember what happened to him. He felt it now and he saw it unfold in front of him. His eyes closed and reopened in front of the office building. Things were different. He could see the streets and the city around him. The city that was now blocked off by this wall of clouds was home. The vision took over completely. He could see another version of himself, nervous and sweating, wrapped within a trench coat. Felix watched his body enter the office building from the front door. He followed. Felix watched himself move to the center of the lobby. He kneeled down to the floor and clenched his hands together. The swarming workers in business suits moved around him. Some were irritated by him blocking their way. Felix approached his double. He placed his hand on his shoulder. The double stood up and removed the coat. Packs of dynamite were strapped to his chest. A mess of colored wires and electrical tape surrounded his rib cage. His right hand held a remote detonator. Felix was in shock, the double opened his arms and let out a savage cry. The hand thumbed the remote and the building was demolished by a fiery explosion. Felix flew back and fell into pitch darkness. He heard that bitter voice from before.

"There you are, the failure, the fruit of my loins."

Felix felt the anger of his past life. He felt the torture and ridicule.

"You took her from me; my love and my life."

Years and years of that voice returned. He screamed uncontrollably as he tasted the medicine. Prescribed pills were forced down his throat, almost triple the dosage.

"So I will deny you your own."

The vision was broken as he found himself moving through the wall of clouds and falling over a cliff of broken concrete, leading down into some kind of empty void. Felix had no control over his body. Vespertine watched him touch the wall of clouds. His body was pulled inside the fog. His shadow twitched and then began to fall over the edge. She grabbed his limp body and pulled him back up. Felix opened his eyes slightly to see the abyss beneath him. A bottomless pit of thunder and lightning. The office building and restaurant were sitting on some kind of island. They were cut off by clouds with no real way off. They were truly trapped, he thought. The voice continued.

"Give me that. I'll show you the real way. I will show you how a man does it."

Felix felt the body hit the floor. He did not see it. His father fell to the floor of their old home. He blamed himself for both of their deaths.

They both fell backwards onto the street. The fog swam and moved around them. Bolts of lightning surrounded their tired bodies. Vespertine rose to see Felix curled into a ball, shivering. She felt a shock. Her eyesight disappeared. The island and wall of fog vanished to a man and woman, early twenties, walking through the crowds of a busy street. The picture moved closer to reveal their faces. Both the man and the woman are beautiful and striking. She rested her head on his shoulder. Vespertine felt time move. Trees and leaves fell away and withered to the changing of seasons. The man and woman changed. Their complections worsened, their eyes grew red and swollen. Scabs appeared across the faces and hands. She watched the couple make love passionately. When they were finished, their faces grew spiteful and ugly. They fought so desperately once they left their bed.

Vespertine felt the warmth of tears over her face. She could not close her eyes. The man and woman grew weary and tired as the fighting continued. The man scaled to the top of some building, the one with the fancy restaurant across the street. It was the same one they used to go to on Saturday nights. He looked at her and said that he wanted to know if someone with nothing to hold onto could fly. He jumped off. The woman followed. Vespertine watched herself hit the ground. Her body splattering across pavement with grim finality. She watched herself die. The vision broke away and faded into the fog. Felix moved far away from her, in the corner of the street, his feet dangling over the edge of the island. He wanted to let himself slide over the edge. To fall into oblivion. He thought of where it may lead him. Vespertine slowly crawled to his side. She let her feet fall over the edge. Her hand clutched his.

"What did you see?" she asked.

"I saw what happened to me, why I'm here, what this place is." Felix said.

She looked up.

"Tell me," she pleaded.

Felix looked at her green eyes, then returned his gaze to the abyss, he couldn't look at her anymore. He missed the ignorance of not knowing the truth.

"My mother died in childbirth. My father hated me. They married young and they wanted to enjoy life together. I took that away from him. He decided to make me suffer for as long as I had to. I was always depressed. Maybe it was inherited from my mother. My father made me see a therapist. I had to pay for my own sessions. I made a bomb when I was eighteen. Every weekend, I would add to it, make it bigger and stronger. No one knew, not even my father. I got an office job, data entry. I was twenty one. Despite this, he never let up. It went on forever; the abuse, both verbal and physical. His drinking got worse and worse as time went on. When I made enough money, I was going to scare my father, I wanted him to leave me alone, I wanted him to call me a man and leave me be. I bought some pills and took them to the house. I threatened to take them all. He was drunk. He knew that I was lying, that I was afraid. He took the pills, and he downed every single one. He said that it was my fault. I lost control, whatever control I had left then. I took my pills too. All of them. I drove to work and I blew myself up along with the building."

Vespertine was silent.

"I know you hate me now, I'm so sorry. Don't leave me. Don't leave me in this hell."

She wrapped her arms around him and spoke.

"My husband and I were addicts, too. It was something we did for fun, for recreation, you know? Soon it became more than fun. It became necessary. We needed it. More than food or water. More than each other. We fought constantly. Punching, kicking and scratching each other. He ran away from me a few times. But I always found him, settled in and took his score. He wanted to get away from me so badly. I wouldn't let it happen, I needed him. This happened for years. We had been together since we were fifteen. We were twenty four now. We could not move on. Move past the pain we tried to silence. One day after we lost our apartment to a fire. He climbed the office building near our block. He jumped. I could not speak. I couldn't even breathe. I just followed him."

"I'm so sorry," Felix said.

"Me too."

Felix wanted to hold her tighter, to kiss her. But a voice called her name, she looked back and her face lit up. She got up and ran towards the man. It was her husband. He did not have to question that. He looked back enough to see two shadows embrace. Felix remained at the edge of the world, feet dangling, waiting for the right moment to fall. He thought about everything he had seen around him. He woke up in hell and now he found himself in limbo. Some kind of purgatory? It was a place between heaven and hell where he could do nothing but watch and wander. He thought of the fortunate ones in the restaurant. They were so full of joy, no worries, no guilt. The men in white, they had to be angels, just like the people who dined in luxury behind unbreakable glass. They held the answers. Felix began to wonder if he had been led in this direction. Not by Vespertine. But by something else. He wanted to know. An elderly man moved slowly to the edge and sat down next to Felix.

"You don't look like the others," the old man said.

"You are young."

"Am I?" Felix replied.

He didn't know what else to say.

"What do you want?" asked Felix.

"How did you get here, young man?"

"We escaped from the building. I wanted to leave this place. I want to go home. Do you know how to leave this place?"

"None of us do, but we all want to go home, son. Sometimes you have to take what you can get," said the elder.

"There's not much to take here."

Felix grew tired of the conversation. He looked back at Vespertine, sitting with her man down the street.

"Did she run with you?"

"She did," said Felix.

"You shouldn't worry," the elder chuckled.

"People always grow sick of each other, especially when in close quarters. She'll come back to you, and it will be up to you what to do then."

"What do you mean?" asked Felix.

"I mean that it's your choice. That's all we have left. You can choose to look at the people in the windows. You can fall over the edge here and find out what happens to you then. Or you can go back into your building and stay there."

"Go back?" Felix was confused.

"You said that you escaped?"

"Yes..."

"How do you know they didn't just let you leave?" Felix furrowed his brow and looked up. The elder smiled with crooked teeth.

Felix didn't know. He just wanted to escape. He didn't remember that he watched his father die, that he destroyed himself and an entire office building. He didn't know that he was a coward, and a murderer. Now that he did, He wasn't sure of what to do. He wanted to know why he was in this place. Why there was no fire, no burning or torture, just a building and a street that leads to nowhere. Felix looked at the building. When he turned around, the old man was still smiling. He got up and walked towards the building, before leaving the old man he turned around.

"Did you ever fall off the edge?"

"I have," the elder muttered.

"What happens?"

"You end up back here," the elder shrugged and slowly rolled over the edge and into the unknown.

Felix turned and walked to the building, he swept his hand across the concrete. It felt real. It had to be his old workplace. He remembered everything; the sights and smells of busy people, the loud barrage of commuters. The city was alive and breathing and he enjoyed living within that microcosm of the world. Felix looked up and down at the pillars of stone. He felt unturned memories come back. He remembered the architecture of the building and the times he went over blueprints with some of the other employees. One of his jobs was to convert the data from scratches of paper into the computer. Felix wanted to return to the building. He thought of entering the door he and Vespertine had come from.

There were too many stairs to climb up again. He would lose the energy he had regained resting on the street. He went over the curves and shoulders of the building again. He recalled the little known maintenance shaft that the builders used to transport supplies and materials from the top floor to the ground level.

Felix wanted to know what was at the top. There was something at the bottom. There had to be something worth seeing at the top. He slowly stepped back into the building. He went through the front door. The lobby where he had detonated the bomb. It was empty. He took careful steps through the hall. Flashes of the explosion ran through his head. He felt overwhelming sadness. Not for him, for the others. The innocent. Minding their own business, when this madman enters the building and changes their lives. Ends their lives. Felix knew that he was beyond forgiveness, but he wanted to do so much to take back what he had done. To save those people. To let them live and allow only him to die. He turned the corner before the elevators and ducked behind the receptionist's desk.

Several of the men in white had gathered in a group. They stood silent in the corner. Felix edged around the desk and saw the enclave near the fire exit. The opening to the shaft was inside there. The men in white were not moving. He wanted to avoid making noise. There was too much distance between the desk and enclave to sneak. He decided to make a run for it. He would only get one chance before he'd be caught. He took off and ran into the enclave and bounced back to the floor. The covering was hard, unable to bust through on his own. Felix looked to his left to see the fire extinguisher and to his right to see the men in white approaching.

The men grabbed Felix and threw him to the ground, they were aggressive. They were the negative, the opposite of the men in the office. Felix was thrashed by the suited angels. His wounds healed and his clothes mended themselves as he struggled to his feet. They were trying to establish dominance, to make him go willingly. One of them spoke after minutes of violent action.

"Please sir, come with us," they said.

Felix lured them to the desk. They bottlenecked into the space behind the desk and reached for his feet, they began to drag him to the elevator, the white doors opened and Felix pulled his legs desperately. He rolled out of the angel's grasp and dived for the fire extinguisher, with a rolling motion he threw it through the enclave, it burst into white smoke and he dove through the opening made. The angels fought their way through the opening.

They were too large to fit at first. The angels were enraged, ripping and tearing at concrete with bare hands. Felix looked up to see the shaft. He went through the small office door and barricaded himself away from the angels. All that was left was to begin the ascent. Felix remembered climbing the rungs from floor to floor after hours. He stopped to think of Vespertine, her sitting in the street with her man. Would she have come with him to this place? Fighting the furious angels? As time went on, Felix began to feel less regard for his own body as his wounds healed on their own. He lost any fear in falling as he began to climb the rungs to the top floor.

Climbing was somehow easier than the descent down the staircase, perhaps because Felix was not afraid of what could await him. He simply needed to know what this place was. He felt weightless as he scrambled up the rungs to the top floor. He climbed further and further, his mind wondered. There were moments where he thought he heard echoes of voices, calling him. He put them out of his mind. He wondered if they were the voices of the office. Felix worried whether the men in white or the skulls of the workers would make their way into the shaft and attack him. He put that thought out of his mind. He wanted her back. Why couldn't she stay with him? He hoped that she found some kind of happiness with the husband she once had.

Felix looked up as he climbed and could see the end of the shaft. He was almost on the top floor. It was near the end of his journey. He slowed his climb as he began to hyperventilate. He rested before climbing through the trapdoor into the top floor. For some reason, he thought of his parents. He was filled with sorrow, with regret. He opened the door and pulled himself up onto the surface above. He rose to see the enormous white room. The top floor held groups of tables and chairs. Every inch of the room was filled with men in white suits. There was talking and laughing. Some prayed in silence.

All around the boardroom were beautiful painted portraits of angels and demons. Stained glass windows extended over and around the paintings. He did not see these from outside. This room held vast and amazing architecture. It reminded him of the restaurant below in the streets. He kept himself hidden from sight. He looked all over the room, the ceiling was painted in some kind of renaissance style. The figures sat around a table, there was a man in the center who looked to the ground, the others were off in their own worlds, arguing and conversing. Somehow all focus was placed on the man in the center. At the very end of the room, there was a staircase that led to a door behind a massive waterfall that flowed into small rivulets that outlined the room itself.

Felix began to move quickly and quietly behind the pillars, trying to find a way to get to the door. He wanted to know what was behind the door. He felt compelled to enter the door. Something was leading him to open the door. As he prepared to move across the floor to the next pillar, there was some kind of commotion with the men in white. Something had startled them.

They all rose from their seats at the round tables and swarmed to the open door that Felix had entered from. They picked up on his presence. He would soon be found. There would be no way out, then. Whatever they decide to do would be final. There were too many to escape from, to fight off. He scrambled towards the waterfall. The men in white began to transform. Their suit jackets ripped open to reveal looming white wings as they flew one after the other down the shaft. They were magnificent angels. Felix stumbled through the waterfall and climbed his way to the staircase. The stairs themselves were made of falling water. He slipped and fell, angry at first, then calm as he ascended the obstacle. He placed one foot against the wall and slowly pushed his body up the wall diagonally. The ancient door was above him. He held still against the wall and inched forward until he reached his hand out to the door. He turned the knob and pushed himself through.

Felix's lungs screamed for air. The climb had drained him of his energy. His black tailored clothes dried themselves. The water pushed out of the threads and left a large puddle on the carpet beneath him. The texture was familiar. It was that of the office. The sight of the carpet frightened him and he sat up to see the same office he found himself again an eternity ago. Felix was overwhelmed with emotion. This was all a loop. He felt defeated, tricked. He crawled into the corner and cowered. Felix waited for the inevitable. He closed his eyes and waited.

Nothing came for him. Felix opened his eyes to see the office. He rose to his feet and began walking through the hall. The cubicles were empty. The hallways led into one main walkway that led down a corridor of white. Felix slowly followed the line until he reached the end of the corridor. There was a single desk against the wall. A man in a crisply tailored white suit sat at the chair. In his hands, a single sheet of paper. The same painting on the ceiling of the board room was on his wall. Felix approached and the man looked up to see him. The man in white did not look surprised. He motioned for Felix to come closer. The entire room was white. The windows were opened and strong gusts of wind and blinding sun entered the room. Felix felt peaceful vibes from the man. He rose from his chair and began to speak.

"Hello, my son, how can I help you?"

Felix was unsure of what to say. There was so much to know. How to begin? How to prepare for the answers?

"Who are you? Why am I here? What the hell is this place?"

The man in white smiled.

"I have no name, friend. Names are unimportant in this place. The soul is what matters, the memory of who you were holds more importance than who you are now. You are here because of your actions, and ironically, Hell would be the correct descriptor."

"So this is Hell?"

"It is a form of hell."

"A form? You mean there are others?" asked Felix.

"There is a form for all who enter. The rooms change their colors, their textures to fall in line with their actions. This is obviously the form decided for you."

"Decided?" asked Felix.

"Chosen by the rooms. Chosen to suit you and your needs. Do you recall what you have done to get here? The rooms made this for you because quite simply, it is what you think of more than anything else."

Felix paused for a moment.

"Who decided this?"

"The rooms, my friend."

"Why?"

"Because this is the process. We keep the environment peaceful and maintain the workload for those involved to keep it running."

"Keep it running?"

"This is a business of souls, son. However a sinful creature decides to end it's life, we are assigned with the task of maintaining the medium of confession and repentance for that soul. It is this confession and acceptance that perpetuates this place. It is the same for you and for all others like you. For the souls affected by their actions, the rooms shall form your place of penance. It is the same for all who hold sin before us. For you? You exploded a building and a small restaurant on a city street. All those you've affected are out there with you."

"You mean, all those people I killed?" Felix asked.

The angel looked forlorn.

"Indeed. Your sin is the source of much sorrow and pain. The source carries a pain much heavier than your own. The building we stand in was taken from your memories. Those with sin were placed here. They have been given the opportunity to repent for their own mistakes, rather than punish those without mercy. We provide an option for salvation."

"Salvation? But I saw them. They were crying, screaming." Felix became furious at the angel's arrogance.

"They were being sucked into those computer screens. Their skin was pulled off their bodies. Your words made them suffer. You tried to do the same to me." he said.

"Their injuries were sustained by your foolish decisions. The words from those screens are taken from their own subconscious minds. They are the things they feared the most. Like you, they are facing whatever dark secrets they hold beneath the skin. You still remain in denial."

Felix was taken aback. He had already known what he'd seen.

"And the people outside of the building?" he asked.

"The people on the streets remain there. They are innocent and unknowing. Consider them encased within their own form of purgatory. Some choose to remember and accept what has happened to them. Some still believe they are alive. They will continue to aimlessly walk the same path over and over. Some believe that this is a dream. Like you, they believe they will soon wake up and will have a chance to live any way they please. But this is not the truth."

"And what is the truth!?" Felix shouted.

"The truth is, those in the restaurant are not like you. They are the rooms. The rooms are without sin, without imperfection. The rooms create your place of penance and they provide the illusion of a heaven. It is something to worship. The rooms have given you something to desire. It was made to instill a need to escape. They have given you and the rest of them hope, to make them feel alive."

Felix was outraged.

"Why would you do that? And what are these rooms?!"

The angel began to show some emotion. He began to sound human as his voice raised;

"To take it from you. It is necessary to remove all hope, all doubt of the rooms. This is your creation. This is what you made and you deserved to see all of it. This is your home. It is integral to your confession, to your repentance. You think you're the only one to have gone through this? They all ran to the streets, desperately trying to find some sort of escape. They realized the truth, and they returned. As did you."

"I'm not going to join them," Felix said defiantly.

"You have the choice to stay outside. You are free to wander without meaning or purpose. But make no mistake, the road is finite. Your judgment will be here, in the rooms. The rooms are creation. They are God. They will wait for you. They have no sense of time. The crimes committed must have their punishment. How exactly it is served, is up to you."

Felix thought of Vespertine. He prayed to be back in her arms, trading notes between cubicles, keeping the facade of life running strong.

"She is just like you. She ran from her truth. She committed more sin, against you. Left alone for one who did not return her feelings. You should know that she followed you here. She made the choice and returned to her place within the rooms."

Felix made the connection. The angels in the boardroom were attacking her. She must have been the voices from within the elevator shaft. He longed to be back at that moment. What he wouldn't give to could fall back to her. They could be together. Something sharp pierced his chest when he asked the question.

"She died by my hand as well?" asked Felix.

"The building exploded as she and her husband fell back to the earth. You are all connected by your sin. Understand that your memories will keep this place standing. You cannot destroy the rooms. You cannot run from your memories. You have killed so many. The rooms will sustain. The rooms will continue."

"But that means I could leave this place?"

"The man who stepped over the edge was right. You may exit the building but the rooms, you cannot leave."

Felix did not understand.

"What rooms?"

The man in white pointed to the windows.

"The rooms have made this. This is where you belong. There is no other place. The rooms will not deny you of your creation. This is your gift. This is your special hell."

Felix lowered himself to the floor, he felt his heart leave his body. There was no hope. No escape from this place. He was right. Felix fought the logic, but the angel was right. He had created this place. He had hurt all those people. He had hurt Vespertine. More than cause hurt, he had killed them. He had taken their lives in the wake of his torture and suffering.

"What do I have to do?"

"You already know the answer to the question. Continue to wander, if you must. Accept what you have done. Confess. Repent. Lose that precious piece of humanity that remains. The rooms have you now. It is over. This is the reason our business exists. There is no fire. There are no demons with tridents. There are no kingdoms of clouds. There is nothing but the rooms. The rooms are you. They are shaped by your choices. They are your memory. They are your mistakes."

Felix thought of his parents. He wanted to see them again. He wished for so many more chances. He would be denied. Felix was caught within the rooms. The damned tortured themselves within. The lost wandered the wastelands. The pure were rewarded with peace of mind. The angel stepped forward and offered his hand. Felix felt the tears pouring from his eyes. He took the hand of the angel. His body disappeared. The room had dissolved into the white screen. He would confess. He would repent. There was nothing left. It was the only choice. There was so much pain. There was nothing but time. Felix would redeem her. He would redeem them all. He would redeem himself. Felix emptied his mind and began to speak as the black text of the computer began to appear. There was only a simple phrase.

"Don't belong..."

Fiction:

The Black Eclipse
Book one of the Paavo Harker Mystery

Wasteland Heart
Book two of the Paavo Harker Mystery

Revenant Sun

Stories and poems:

Diamond Blood

The Outsider

Distortion Dreams

The Rooms Have You Now

"tell them about the revolving doors..."

coming soon:
the whispers in the water.

Thank you.